FOR FRANCES
—K.B., —T.B.

Text copyright © 1999 by Kate Banks

Pictures copyright © 1999 by Tomek Bogacki

All rights reserved

Distributed in Canada by Douglas & McIntyre Ltd.

Color separations by Hong Kong Scanner Art

Printed in the United States of America

Art direction and design by Monika Keano

First edition, 1999

Second printing, 1999

Library of Congress Cataloging-in-Publication Data

Banks, Kate, 1960–

The bird, the monkey, and the snake in the jungle/

story by Kate Banks: pictures by Tomek Bogacki

p.   cm.

"A Frances Foster book"

"A rebus book"

Summary: A bird, a monkey, and a snake lose their home in

a tree and go looking for a new home, encountering various jungle

animals on the way. Features rebuses, which are identified with

labels in the margins of the pages.

ISBN 0-374-30729-6

[1. Birds—Fiction.   2. Monkeys—Fiction.   3. Snakes—Fiction.

4. Jungle animals—Fiction.   5. Dwellings—Fiction.   6. Rebuses.]

I. Bogacki, Tomasz, ill. II. Title.

PZ7.B22594B1   1999   98-3860

[E]—dc21

A REBUS BOOK

DESIGNED BY MONIKA KEANO

STORY BY **KATE BANKS**   PICTURES BY **TOMEK BOGACKI**

The BIRD, the MONKEY, and the SNAKE in the JUNGLE

FRANCES FOSTER BOOKS

FARRAR, STRAUS AND GIROUX

NEW YORK

Deep in the

there was a . . .

jungle

tree

At the top
of the
lived a

In the middle
of the
lived a

At the bottom
of the
lived a

This  was their .

In the morning

when the  came out, the

would sing.

The

who was sleeping

on a

below

would cry,

"Quiet. I am trying to sleep."

At lunchtime

the

would

eat

he had

picked

from

the .

He would

toss the

down on

the back

of the

"The sky is falling,"

the

would cry.

"It's just the 🐵," the 🐦 would screech.

"Stop that racket," the 🐦 would shout. But the 🐍 kept on dancing.

In the evening when the 🌙 came out, the 🐍 would begin to dance around the 🌳.

sun
bird
monkey
branch
nuts
tree
shells
snake
moon

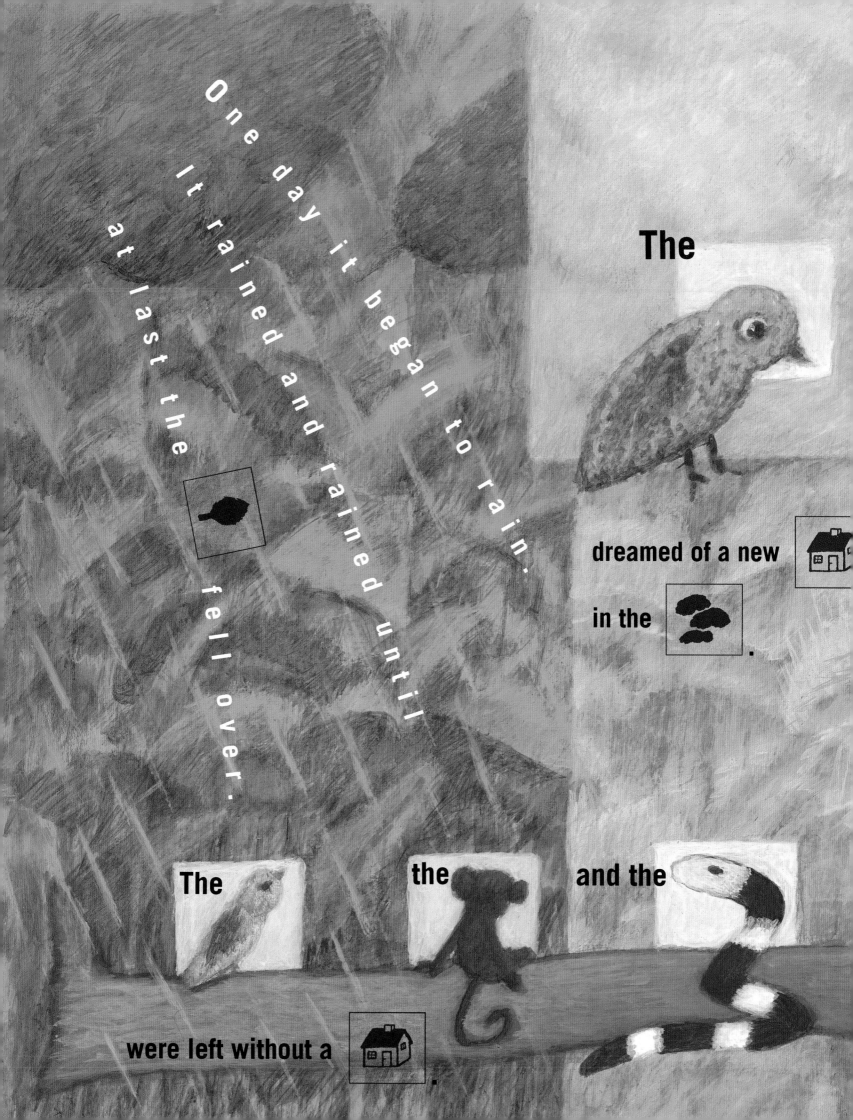

One day it began to rain.

It rained and rained and rained until at last the fell over.

The dreamed of a new in the .

The the and the were left without a .

The dreamed of a new with hanging from the .

And the dreamed of a new with growing up to the .

And each of them dreamed of a of his very own.

tree

bird

monkey

snake

home

clouds

bananas

windows

ferns

door

The  the 🐒

and the 🐍 "No, mine,"

said

the

followed the 🌧️

deeper into the 🌴.

At the first 🍃

they came to, **the**

said,

"That will be mine."

bird

monkey

"I don't see

why it won't be

mine,"

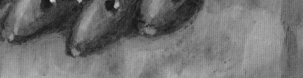
snake

said

the

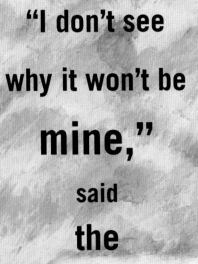

"Because it's ours,"

came a voice

from

inside the 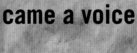 .

path

jungle

tree

squirrel

And out leaped a big

with seven little .

squirrels

Next the

the

and the

came to a

with

hanging from the .

"**How beautiful,**"

said

the

flying to the top.

But there was

a

with eight  in it.

bird

monkey

snake

tree

flowers

branches

nest

eggs

The [bird] the [monkey] and the [worm] kept on moving.

The next [leaf] they came to was full of [bats].

"No room here," they said.

Night fell.

The  came out.

 began to sparkle in the sky.

There were strange noises in the .

The the

and the

stopped to sleep.

bird

monkey

snake

tree

bats

moon

stars

jungle

"It is dark," said the

"It is cold," said the

"And scary," said the

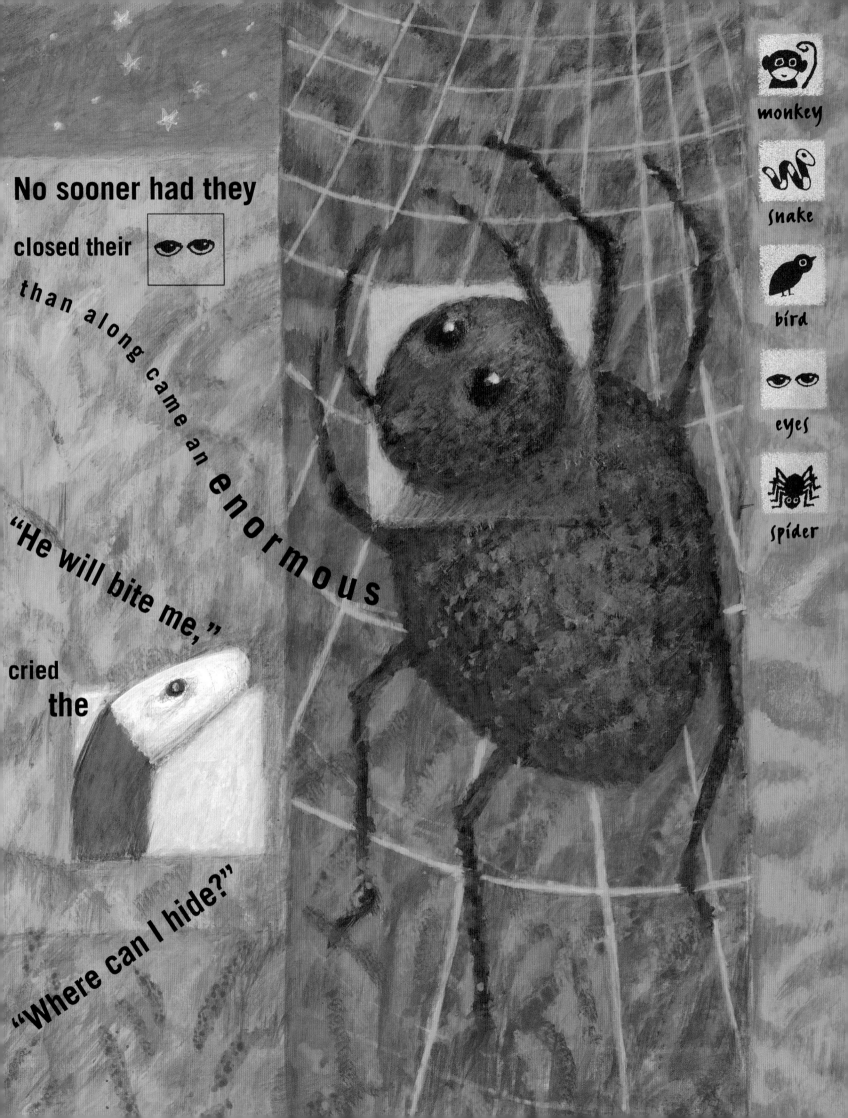

No sooner had they

closed their 👀

than along came an **enormous**

"He will bite me,"

cried the

"Where can I hide?"

monkey

snake

bird

eyes

spider

But soon the  heard a strange rustling in the  .

It was a

"He will eat me,"  cried the

monkey

nuts

hand

spider

bushes

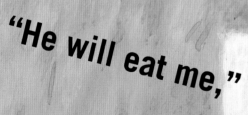
crocodile

"No, he won't,"

said

the

And she

flew down

close to the

and screeched

into his ear.

They had just
gotten back
to sleep
when
the
heard
a growling
noise.

"It's a

she cried.

"He will eat me!"

"I'll take care of him,"
said the

And he
began to
slither
closer
and
closer
to the

until the

r a n a w a y.

bird

crocodile

tiger

snake

In the morning

when the came up,

the  the

and the

set out again to look for a new

.

They came to a

with great

green .

At the bottom there was a

"Is there room for us?"

asked the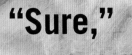

"Sure,"

said the

"If you don't mind my croaking."

"Not at all," said the

"Croak all you want," said the

"The more the better," said the

So they moved into the big .

sun

bird

monkey

snake

home

tree

leaves

frog

Each day the

sang

as the  came up.

The

threw on the

and the .

When the came out,

the

danced.

And

the

croaked all day long.

And they were very happy.